To ADDISON!
ALL THE BEST!
♡/ B. Lee

To my mother, Paula, who has always encouraged me
to follow my dreams wherever they may take me—B.L.

Printed in the United States of America
First Edition
1 3 5 7 9 10 8 6 4 2
ISBN 978-1-4231-6757-0
F322-8368-0-13135
Library of Congress Card Catalog Number: 2013931926
Designed by Winnie Ho
Visit www.disneybooks.com

THE LITTLE MERMAID

Part of Their World

by Elle D. Risco   illustrated by Brittney Lee

Disney PRESS
New York

"No peeking!"
Ariel told her friend Flounder.

She darted around, trying to find
the perfect spot. Then she dug a hole
and hid a shell, smoothing sand over it.

"Ready!"
she called.

Flounder was usually good at Treasure Hunt.

But this time, he kept looking in the wrong places.

"Colder, colder,"
Ariel said, giggling.

Flounder pulled something out of the sand.
"Then what is *this*?"

It was shiny like a shimmery shell.

It was smooth—even smoother than a stone tossed and tumbled by the surf.

It was long and thin like sea grass . . . except for a funny round part at the end.

Ariel had never seen anything like it under the sea.

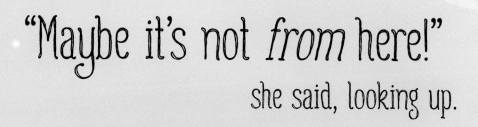

"Maybe it's not *from* here!"

she said, looking up.

She swam in circles, trying to picture the world
she'd only heard about.

A world of air, not water . . .
a world of bright light, not deep blue . . .
a world of two-legged creatures called humans.

Ariel wondered what humans used the thing for. "Maybe it's some kind of key to a secret treasure!"

"Or for playing human music!" Flounder suggested.

BONK!

BONK!

BONK!

Ariel waved the object around.
"It's a magic wand!"

She and Flounder brought it to Sebastian.

"It's just a spoon," he said. "Humans use it to eat their food. You must get rid of it. You know how your father feels about the surface."

Ariel frowned.
She couldn't help it that part of the human
world had found its way under the sea.

Then she realized there must be more treasures to find. . . .

"It's a bubbler ubbler!

A lacy dacey!

A braidette!"

Ariel swam over to her sisters.
She showed them what she'd found.
"Aren't they amazing?"

"What are you doing with those . . .
human things?" Aquata shrieked.
"You know we aren't supposed to talk
about the surface."

"Besides, I bet they use that for capturing mermaids," Alana said.

"And that for smushing fish,"
Andrina noted.

"And that for . . . for . . . summoning witches!" Adella finished.

Ariel looked at her sisters. None of them had been to the surface. "Can humans really be so terrible?"

"YES!" It was Ariel's father.

"You must never go to the surface," he warned. "Humans are dangerous. And you should not collect objects from their world."

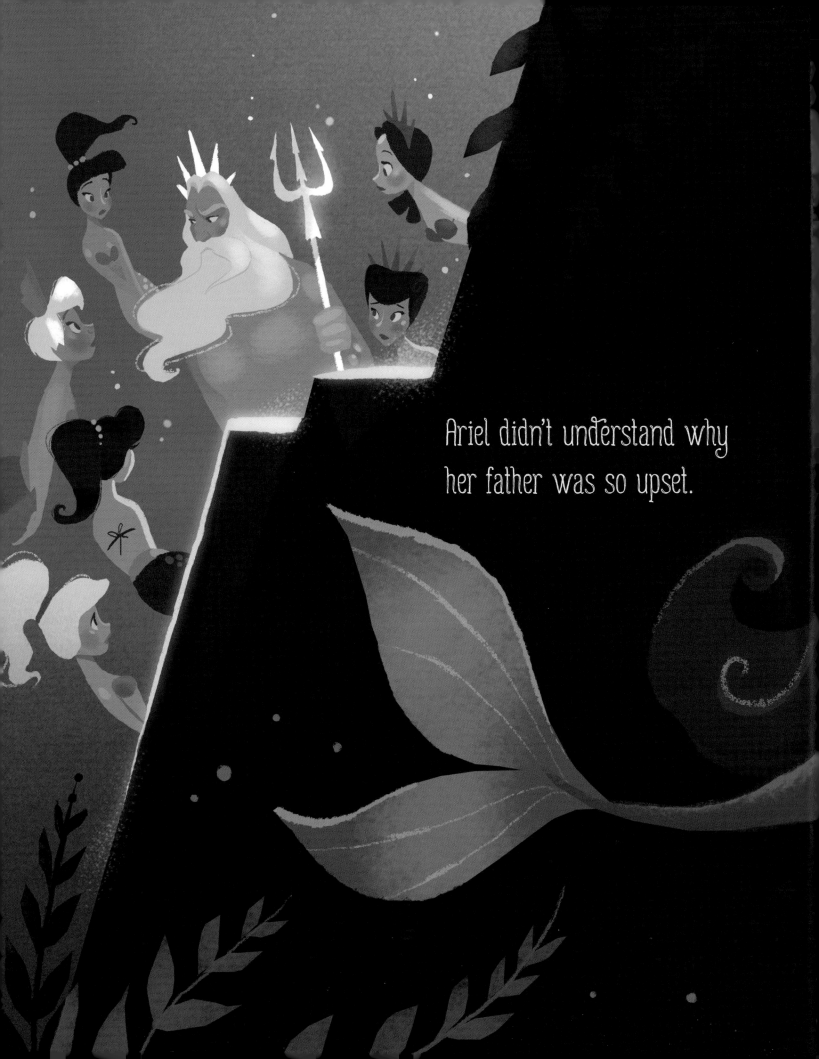

Ariel didn't understand why
her father was so upset.

What if he was wrong about humans?
Would it be so bad if she kept her treasures for a little while?

Ariel and Flounder began another search—
this time for a place to keep everything.
They darted into a narrow rock tunnel.

Then they stumbled into a cavern with glittering walls that stretched up, up, up . . .

"What is this place?" Flounder whispered.

Ariel smiled.

"It's . . . it's . . . it's . . . perfect.
This will be our
secret grotto!"

They looked for more treasures.
Soon they came upon a human necklace.

Hanging from the sparkling chain was
a single perfect pearl.

"Look!" Ariel said to Flounder. "Humans think part of our world is so beautiful they wear it. They can't really be so terrible.

I just knew it."

Maybe someday, she thought,
I'll be able to find out for myself. . . . .